To Laura P. and Emily-Rose S.

Other Baby Bear books to share:

Hold Tight!
The Big Baby Bear Book
Again!
Number One, Tickle Your Tum
The Bear Went Over the Mountain
Oh Where, Oh Where?

First edition for the United States published in 2003
by Barron's Educational Series, Inc.

First published in Great Britain in 2003 by
The Bodley Head Children's Books, Random House,
20 Vauxhall Bridge Road, London, SW1V 2SA

Text and illustrations copyright © John Prater 2003

All inquiries should be addressed to:
Barron's Educational Series, Inc.
250 Wireless Boulevard
Hauppauge, New York 11788
http://www.barronseduc.com

Library of Congress Catalog Card No.: 2002116523
International Standard Book No.: 0-7641-5668-3

Printed in Singapore
9 8 7 6 5 4 3 2 1

Is It Christmas?

JOHN PRATER

BARRON'S

"Is it Christmas?" asked Baby Bear, early one morning.
"No, not yet," said Grandbear, "but after two more
sleeps, it will be."
Baby Bear finished breakfast and bounced
downstairs to help Grandbear.

On the mat were lots of cards.
They opened them up
and hung them on ribbons.

Then Baby Bear made lovely cards to send
to all their family and friends.

They scrubbed
and polished the
whole house.

Baby Bear was
a big help!

Then they baked lots of cookies and cakes. "Why are we making so many?" asked Baby Bear.

"They're for our special Christmas visitors," said Grandbear.

What a busy day! Soon, it was bedtime again.

"Is it Christmas?" asked Baby Bear, early the next morning. "Are our visitors here?"
"Soon," said Grandbear, "after one more sleep it will be Christmas, and they'll be here."

"We're going
to bring in
the tree today,"
said Grandbear.
"A tree? Inside
the house?"
laughed Baby Bear.
"Of course," said Grandbear, "our Christmas tree."
But when they opened the door,
they both gasped.

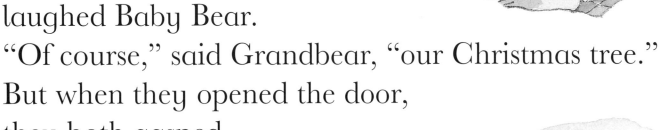

"It's all white!" shouted Baby Bear.
"I thought it might snow," said Grandbear.

"Wow!" said Baby Bear, running outside,

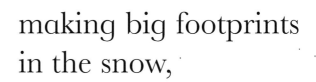

making big footprints in the snow,

and catching snowflakes.

Grandbear joined in the fun.

They threw snowballs at each other.
Grandbear seemed to miss every time . . .

. . . but Baby Bear didn't.

Then they rolled some very big snowballs and made a jolly snowbear.

Baby Bear got a
lift to the top of
the hill,

and a ride all the way down. Wheeeeee!

"Now then, let's find our Christmas tree," said Grandbear.

"This one?" asked Baby Bear.
"That's far too big," said Grandbear.

"This one?" asked Baby Bear.
"That's much too small," said Grandbear.

"... But this one is just right."

Grandbear dug it up, and carried it home,
wondering why it felt so heavy.

Grandbear dragged the tree indoors.

Baby Bear helped
to plant it in
a great big pot.

"Do we climb up it now?" asked Baby Bear.
"No, we do something that's better
than that," said Grandbear.

"We decorate it."

They
decorated
the tree from
top to bottom,
and then
the rest of
the room.
"Wow!" said
Baby Bear.

"There's just one more
thing . . ." said Grandbear.

". . . the lights!"
"Oooh," said Baby Bear, "they're like
twinkly stars!"

It all looked so wonderful that Baby Bear didn't want to come to the table for dinner. So they sat by the tree and had a cozy picnic.

"It's Christmas tomorrow," said Grandbear, "and our special visitors will be here."

"That's nice," yawned Baby Bear, sleepily.

"Just one more sleep," whispered Grandbear.

Later that night, while Baby Bear slept, someone left some presents under the Christmas tree.

"Is it Christmas?"
asked Baby Bear,
early the next
morning.
"Yes it is!" said
Grandbear.

"YIPPEE!"
shouted
Baby Bear.

There was a loud knock at the front door.
"Listen, they're here!" said Grandbear.
"Who?" asked Baby Bear.
"Our special visitors," said Grandbear.
"Who?" asked
Baby Bear again.

"The whole family," said Grandbear.
"Merry Christmas, Baby Bear!" they shouted.
"Merry Christmas, everyone!" said Baby Bear.